Pick a perfect Pumpkin

Learning about Pumpkin Harvests

by Robin Koontz

Illustrated by Nadine Takvorian

PICTURE WINDOW BOOKS
a capstone imprint

Special thanks to our adviser for his expertise:

Terry Flaherty, PhD, Professor of English
Minnesota State University, Mankato

Shelly Lyons, editor; Lori Bye, designer
Nathan Gassman, art director; Jane Klenk, production specialist
The illustrations in this book were created digitally and with pencil.

Picture Window Books
151 Good Counsel Drive
P.O. Box 669
Mankato, MN 56002-0669
877-845-8392
www.capstonepub.com

Printed in the United States of America in North Mankato, Minnesota.
032010   005740CGF10

All books published by Picture Window Books
are manufactured with paper containing at least
10 percent post-consumer waste.

Library of Congress Cataloging-in-Publication Data
Koontz, Robin Michal.
Pick a perfect pumpkin : learning about pumpkin harvests / by Robin
Koontz ; illustrated by Nadine Takvorian.
p. cm. — (Autumn)
Includes index.
ISBN 978-1-4048-6011-7 (library binding)
ISBN 978-1-4048-6391-0 (paperback)
1. Pumpkin—Harvesting—Juvenile literature. I. Takvorian, Nadine.
II. Title. III. Series: Autumn (Series)
SB347.K66 2010
635'.62—dc22   2010000906

The autumn air feels cool.
Colorful leaves blow in the breeze.

3

Rows of pumpkins glow under a blue sky.

Pumpkin harvest time is here!

4

Pumpkins probably first grew in North America.
Now they are grown all around the world.

Welcome to our pumpkin farm!

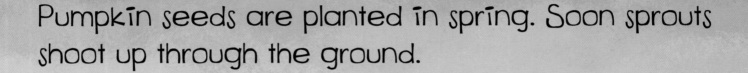

Pumpkin seeds are planted in spring. Soon sprouts shoot up through the ground.

The sprouts grow into long vines. The vines flower. Pumpkins grow from those flowers.

A pumpkin has lots of seeds inside.
Because it has seeds, a pumpkin
is a fruit.

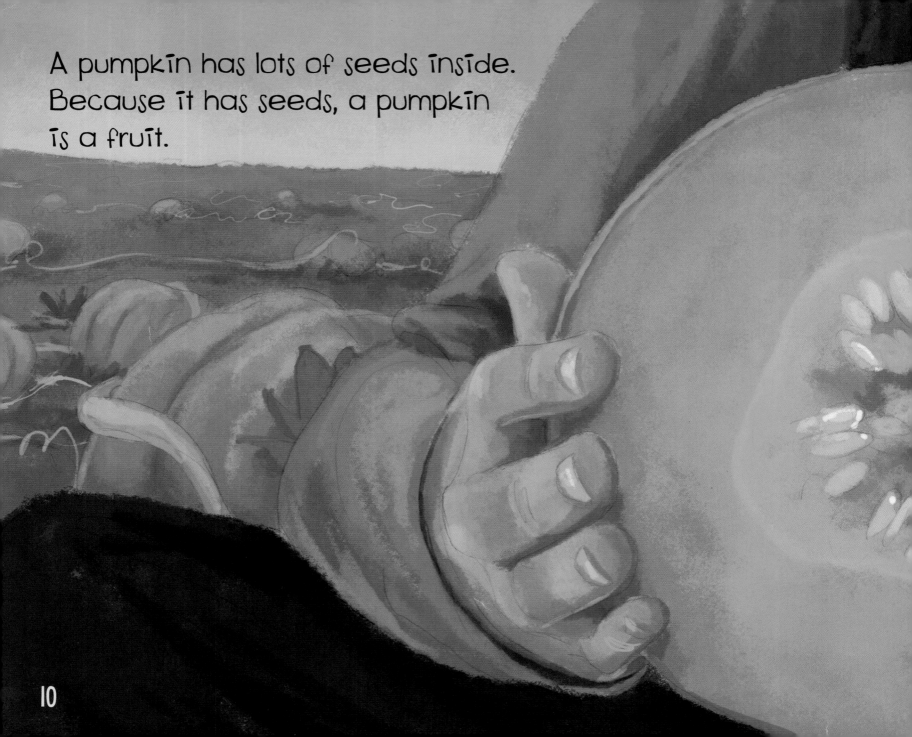

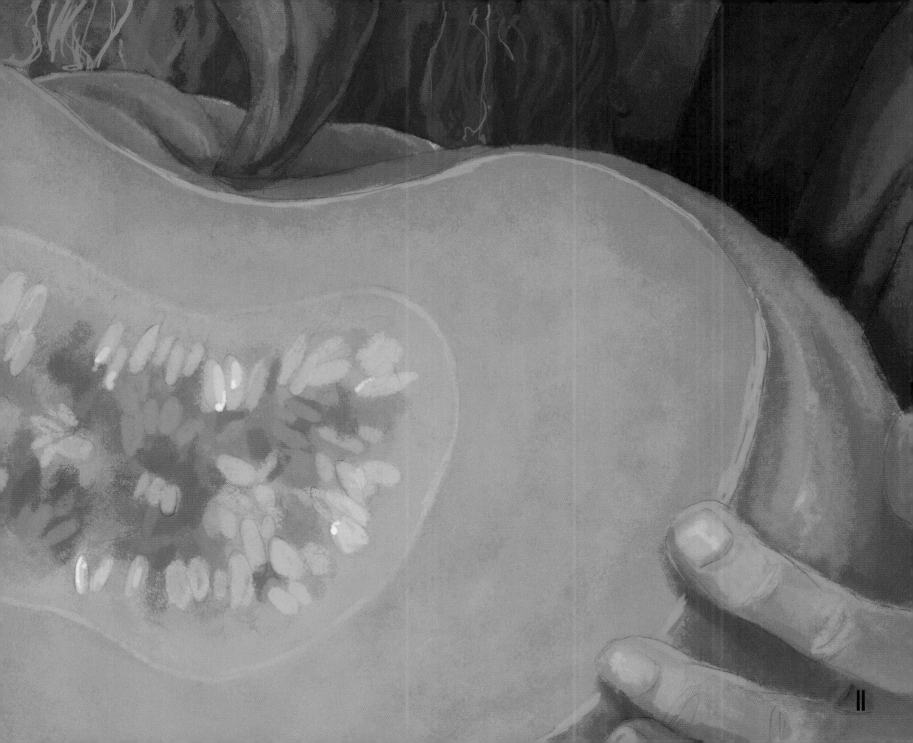

Pumpkins turn colors as they grow.
They can be orange, green, yellow, or white.
Some are even red or blue.

Pumpkins come in many shapes and sizes.
Some pumpkins can weigh as much as a cow!

15

A ripe pumpkin's color is bold. It sounds hollow when fingers tap it. Once picked, pumpkins should be stored in a cool dry place.

Pumpkins are used to make bread and soup.
They are also used to make pumpkin pie.

19

People carve scary faces in pumpkins.
The jack-o'-lanterns shine bright on Halloween night.

20

21

Pumpkin Critter

What you need:

- craft knife
- one medium-sized pumpkin for the body
- one small pumpkin for the head
- glue gun and glue sticks
- scissors
- sturdy cardboard
- craft paper
- toothpicks
- craft paint and brush

What you do:

1. Ask an adult to use a craft knife to cut the top off the pumpkin body. This makes a flat place to glue the pumpkin head.
2. Ask an adult to cut the bottom off the pumpkin head. This makes a flat place to glue to the pumpkin body.
3. Ask an adult to use a glue gun to glue the pumpkin head to the pumpkin body.
4. Let the glue dry.
5. Using a scissors, cut a heart shape out of cardboard. The heart will be the critter's feet.
6. Using a glue stick, glue the pointed end of the heart to the bottom of the pumpkin body.
7. Cut out ears, arms, and a tail from the craft paper.
8. Fold the edges of the body parts. Using a glue stick, glue the edges to the body and head.
9. Poke in toothpicks for whiskers on the critter's face.
10. Paint eyes, a nose, and a mouth.

Glossary

autumn—the season of the year between summer and winter; autumn is also called fall

harvest time—the time of year when fruits and vegetables are ready for picking

jack-o'-lantern—a pumpkin with a painted or carved face

North America—the continent in the Western Hemisphere that includes the United States, Canada, Mexico, and Central America

ripe—ready to pick and eat

sprout—a young plant that has just appeared above the soil

stem—the part of the plant from which the leaves and pumpkin grow

vine—a plant with a long stem that clings to the ground, a wall, or a fence as it grows

More Books to Read

Dolbear, Emily J. *How Did That Get to My Table? Pumpkin Pie*. Community Connections. Ann Arbor, Mich.: Cherry Lake Pub., 2010.

Esbaum, Jill. *Seed, Sprout, Pumpkin, Pie*. Picture the Seasons. Washington, D.C.: National Geographic, 2009.

Harris, Calvin. *Pumpkin Harvest*. All about Fall. Mankato, Minn.: Capstone Press, 2008.

Internet Sites

FactHound offers a safe, fun way to find Internet sites related to this book. All of the sites on FactHound have been researched by our staff.

Here's all you do:
Visit *www.facthound.com*
FactHound will fetch the best sites for you!

Index

Check out all the books in the Autumn series:

Apples, Apples Everywhere!: Learning about Apple Harvests

Busy Animals: Learning about Animals in Autumn

Leaves Fall Down: Learning about Autumn Leaves

Pick a Perfect Pumpkin: Learning about Pumpkin Harvests